THE ITCH BOOK

by CRESCENT DRAGONWAGON

illustrated by JOSEPH MAHLER

Macmillan Publishing Company   New York

For Eureka Springs, Arkansas,

the town that has always

scratched my itch

    —C.D.

For Iris,

the Captain,

and Charlie

    —J.M.

Text copyright © 1990 by Crescent Dragonwagon. Illustrations copyright © 1990 by Joseph Mahler.
All rights reserved. No part of this book may be reproduced or transmitted in any form or by any means, electronic or mechanical,
including photocopying, recording, or by any information storage and retrieval system, without permission in writing from the Publisher.
Macmillan Publishing Company, 866 Third Avenue, New York, NY 10022. Collier Macmillan Canada, Inc.
Printed and bound in Singapore. First American Edition   10 9 8 7 6 5 4 3 2 1
The text of this book is set in 14 point Century Expanded. The illustrations are rendered in pen and ink and Prismacolor.

Library of Congress Cataloging-in-Publication Data   Dragonwagon, Crescent. The itch book/by Crescent Dragonwagon;
illustrated by Joseph Mahler. —1st American ed.   p.   cm.   Summary: Relates what happens on a hot day in the Ozarks
when the heat makes everyone itch.   ISBN 0-02-733121-0   [1. Heat — Fiction. 2. Mountain life — Fiction. 3. Stories in rhyme.]
I. Mahler, Joseph, ill. II. Title. PZ8.3.D77It 1990   [E] — dc19   89-2695 CIP AC

Was it
the very first
day
of summer (not some calendar date, but the real
out-of-school 92-degrees-and-not-even-ten-o'clock-yet
summer)
or only still
the last day
of spring?

No matter. You tell me, for
I don't know
but I know this much:
It was *hot*
my, it was hot
hot hot hot
in the Ozark Mountains
heat rising from the ground
shimmering off the trees
sky whitened with sun
and somehow
the itch
begun
that day, began.

Beast and boy and girl
woman man
itchings scratchings
everywhere
in that little tiny town
itchings scratchings
to beat the band
all around,
and on
everyone.

Jeff woke
in his bed
(already
the air
was so still
the white curtain
hanging there
over
the open window
was not moving
even a bit)

and

as he woke Jeff heard

a sound, his hound:

a rattling redbone scrape scrape scrape

paws claws on floor back of ear rolling rubbing

front and rear

against the floor…hear!

It's Reddog scratch scratch scratching

black toenails catching

or trying to catch

an itch

behind an ear.

Was it catching, that itch? Maybe yes,
maybe no, but, natch,
Jeff
had
to scratch
himself
too—
behind his neck.
Heck,
it could have been
a chigger bite,
right? Maybe.

Meanwhile, downstairs,
up early
to beat
the heat
(but there was no retreat, even that early
with the sky bleached muslin white)
Mama was putting up strawberries—
yup, strawberry jam, strawberry jelly.
Well, she (without seeing or hearing
the scratching boy the scratching hound
not yet down and
barely awake upstairs)
felt it too, on her sweat-dripped cheek.
She rinsed off the sugar, reached, scratched
that itch (Sweet, when the nails
find that itching spot! But is it enough?
No, never.)

oh, so hot hot hot
in the red-stained kitchen
where the jelly's cooking
and Mama thought:
     Later—the creek
     soon's I get these berries done
     swimming hole down by the bluff
as Jeff, abed at seven, scratching,
looking at Reddog, thought too:
  Creek.

Papa drives early to Handymart
where he's a clerk
got to scratch that itch
on the way to work
clean shirt clean jeans
outside the window leaves and bushes heated dusty green
Papa nodding to farmers in pickup trucks
oh, he knows everyone
second cup of coffee at the drugstore:
    Mornin', Miz Hardy, gonna be a hot one
    Howdy, Joelda, long time no see
    Glad to be out of school, Joe Paul?
    Your dad got you haulin' hay yet?
And everyone knows Papa, he's always got a nice word to speak
but his knee crease itches bad and it's summer and he's
not immune. He thinks:
    Creek,
    and soon.

And did you see that brown-eyed big-eyed sweet-cream Jersey cow,
over to Berryville?
You think maybe she escaped that need to itch somehow?
No sir, no ma'am, sure as I am
standing here,
she had an itch on her back
bad,
and no way to scratch it
but against
that nice rough cedar post.
Watch her rub
watch her twist her neck
mmmm that bark is good for a cow to scratch on
when a hoof or tail won't do
when it's too hot
to even
moooooooooooooooooo.
    Thank goodness for posts
thinks Jersey-cow Betty
    I'll go down to the creek by and by
    when I'm ready.

And Blaze, the horse on the other bank
whose pasture also fronts the creek—he
gives thanks:
He got an itch so bad his tail won't do it
a tail switch for a scratch? Not a match
for this itch, summer deep
summer hot. Blaze's got a post
himself, but dreams awake:

> Blue water cool water sweet water
> creek.

Even the flies
are itch-bugged: Watch
them rub their wings together,
scratching.

Joelda Calder lifts her hat
scratches her head (imagine that)
Joe Paul his elbow, Papa checks his watch,
sells Fred Hollings a ratchet, Miz Hardy blots her face
with a handkerchief, then even she's got to scratch it.
Fever pitch!
It's hot, we itch, the day's too long!
Something's wrong
but nothing
that a good creek dip
wouldn't
fix....

No one said a word
it wasn't planned
but beast and boy and girl
woman man
as the day grew long and
the evening slow
folks packed up hampers
just happened to go
cold fried chicken
any old thing
not so hot the whippoorwill
didn't sing

whippoorwill whippoorwill
come if you won't
come if you will
through the pasture and down the hill
potato salad T-shirt shorts
moos and neighs and laughs and snorts
pickup trucks and trailer hitches
got to solve those problem itches
drawn like a magnet to that clear water
You want to go? Reckon we oughter.

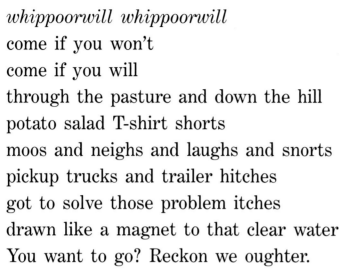

Thrown in
ice cold
delicious *eeeeeeek*
solve the itch:

night picnic
at
King Creek.